the new batch

CUPCAKE DIARIES

Emily's
Cupcake
Chaos!

By Coco Simon
author of Cupcake Diaries

Illustrated by Manuela López

Simon Spotlight
New York   Amsterdam/Antwerp   London
Toronto   Sydney/Melbourne   New Delhi

This book is a work of fiction. Any references to historical events, real people, or real places are used fictitiously. Other names, characters, places, and events are products of the author's imagination, and any resemblance to actual events or places or persons, living or dead, is entirely coincidental.

SIMON SPOTLIGHT
An imprint of Simon & Schuster Children's Publishing Division
1230 Avenue of the Americas, New York, New York 10020
For more than 100 years, Simon & Schuster has championed authors and the stories they create. By respecting the copyright of an author's intellectual property, you enable Simon & Schuster and the author to continue publishing exceptional books for years to come. We thank you for supporting the author's copyright by purchasing an authorized edition of this book.
No amount of this book may be reproduced or stored in any format, nor may it be uploaded to any website, database, language-learning model, or other repository, retrieval, or artificial intelligence system without express permission. All rights reserved. Inquiries may be directed to Simon & Schuster, 1230 Avenue of the Americas, New York, NY 10020 or permissions@simonandschuster.com.
This Simon Spotlight hardcover edition May 2025
© 2025 by Simon & Schuster, LLC
Also available in a Simon Spotlight paperback edition.
All rights reserved, including the right of reproduction in whole or in part in any form.
SIMON SPOTLIGHT and colophon are registered trademarks of Simon & Schuster, LLC.
For information about special discounts for bulk purchases, please contact Simon & Schuster Special Sales at 1-866-506-1949 or business@simonandschuster.com.
Simon & Schuster strongly believes in freedom of expression and stands against censorship in all its forms. For more information, visit BooksBelong.com.
The Simon & Schuster Speakers Bureau can bring authors to your live event. For more information or to book an event, contact the Simon & Schuster Speakers Bureau at 1-866-248-3049 or visit our website at www.simonspeakers.com.
Text by Tracy West • Illustrations by Manuela López • Book design by Brittany Fetcho
The illustrations for this book were rendered digitally.
The text of this book was set in Cardo.
Manufactured in the United States of America 0325 LAK
2 4 6 8 10 9 7 5 3 1
Library of Congress Cataloging-in-Publication Data
Names: Simon, Coco, author. | López, Manuela, 1985– illustrator. | Simon, Coco. Cupcake diaries, the new batch ; 5.
Title: Emily's cupcake chaos! / by Coco Simon ; illustrated by Manuela López.
Description: New York : Simon Spotlight, 2025. | Series: Cupcake diaries the new batch ; 5 | Audience term: Children | Summary: The Mini Cupcake Club friends are excited to bake for the school dance and Emily is determined to provide absolutely perfect cupcakes.
Identifiers: LCCN 2024038245 (print) | LCCN 2024038246 (ebook) | ISBN 9781665971287 (paperback) | ISBN 9781665971294 (hardcover) | ISBN 9781665971300 (ebook)
Subjects: LCSH: Baking—Juvenile fiction. | Friendship—Juvenile fiction. | Perfectionism (Personality trait)—Juvenile fiction. | CYAC: Baking—Fiction. | Friendship—Fiction. | Perfectionism—Fiction.
Classification: LCC PZ7.S60357 Edt 2025 (print) | LCC PZ7.S60357 (ebook) | DDC [Fic]—dc23/eng/20250114
LC record available at https://lccn.loc.gov/2024038245 • LC ebook record available at https://lccn.loc.gov/2024038246

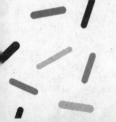

CONTENTS

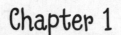

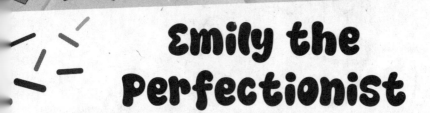

Chapter 1

Emily the Perfectionist

I love ending the school day with soccer practice. I like running fast. I like joking around with my teammates. I like the feeling when I kick the ball and it goes into the goal! There's just one thing I don't like. . . .

"Ugh! I hate how I feel after soccer," I complained to my friend Natalie as we walked home. "I'm such a sweaty mess!"

Natalie laughed. "What are you talking about? You look perfect, as usual."

Then she stopped and stared at my face.

"What?" I asked nervously.

"I was wrong. You do have one hair out of place! Let me fix it. You shouldn't let anyone else see you like that," she answered.

I didn't realize she was joking. I must have looked horrified, because she said, "Emily, I was kidding! You look fine. Great, as always!"

Even though she was kidding, I touched my head, trying to find the stray hair.

Natalie knows me pretty well. When we're baking cupcakes for our club, she has seen me carefully scoop the batter into the mini tins without spilling a drop. She's seen me use a tweezer to put sprinkles on each cupcake, one by one. She knows that I check every cupcake before we pack them up for a client.

I pick out the ones that aren't pretty enough and replace them with better ones.

"People are paying us money for these," I would tell my friends. "They have to be perfect!"

Natalie still hasn't seen *all* of me, though. She doesn't know that I neatly roll my socks and arrange them in a drawer by color.  She didn't see me cry that time I got a 98 on a spelling test instead of 100. She doesn't know that I steam all my shirts to get the wrinkles out.

"Who does that anymore, Emily?" Katie, my stepsister, always asks me. "You're being too hard on yourself."

Is Katie right? I wondered. *Being perfect all the time is exhausting!*

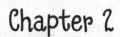

Chapter 2

Not Glitter!

When I got to my dad's house, Katie was at the kitchen table with a bunch of art supplies spread out. I could hear popcorn popping in the microwave.

"Hey, Em, want a snack?" she asked.

"Save me some, please," I replied. "I have to get ready. My mom's coming to pick me up soon."

The popcorn was making the house smell good, so I hurried through my routine.

I'm used to the fact that I live in two different houses now. One is with Katie, my dad, and my stepmom, Sharon. The other one is my mom's place. Sometimes it can get confusing. But I use my calendar to keep track of where I'm supposed to be every day.

I came downstairs with my duffel bag full of clothes and my school backpack. I took a seat in front of the popcorn bowl and grabbed a small handful.

"Whatcha making?" I asked Katie.

"It's Emma's birthday in a few days," Katie began. "Everyone in the Cupcake Club is going to her house for a sleepover. And there's a school dance the next day."

Katie pushed a piece of brown hair behind her ear. I noticed she had a pink

marker stain topped with
glitter on her cheek.

"Emma's favorite color is pink. And I
found this tube of pink glitter with the art
supplies. I just knew I had to make her a
sparkly sign. See?"

As soon as Katie said the word "glitter," my skin began to crawl. Then she held up the sign. It was cute! But the glitter started to drop off right away, getting all over the table.

"Not glitter!" I wailed. I ran to the sink to dampen a paper towel. That was the only way to clean up glitter. That stuff is evil. It gets everywhere!

"You've got glitter and glue on your sweatshirt," I told Katie. "It may never come off."

Katie gazed down. "Oh, yeah! I'm all sparkly."

"That really doesn't bother you?" I asked.

"Nah. You should know by now that I don't mind getting a little messy," Katie said. "I remember when my mom started

dating your dad. I was worried that my mom would like you better because you're like the perfect daughter. Always clean and neat. Everything you do is perfect! And I'm a big mess most of the time." She pointed to her sweatshirt.

Katie had mentioned this before, but I still had trouble believing it.

"And speaking of perfect," Katie said, "I have a business opportunity for the Mini Cupcake Club."

I ignored the last spot of glitter on the table. This was exciting.

"The Cupcake Club was asked to bake cupcakes for the dance. But we want to have fun and not worry about selling cupcakes. It could be a great sales opportunity for your club. What do you think?"

"That would be fantastic! It would be so fun to be at a middle school dance!" I said. "I can't wait to tell everybody!"

I jumped up and hugged Katie.

"I'm counting on you and your friends," Katie said. "Your mini cupcakes have got to be amazing. We raved about you to our principal."

Honk! Honk!

"That's my mom," I said. "Don't worry, our cupcakes will be perfect."

As I headed out the door, I saw that I had pink glitter on my shirt. I took a deep breath.

At least there's no glitter at Mom's house, I thought.

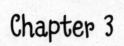

Chapter 3

An Awesome Idea

The next day at lunch, I couldn't wait to tell all my friends about Katie's offer.

"I've got news," I said, sliding into my chair. "Katie is giving us a chance to make cupcakes for her middle school dance."

"No waaaaaaaaaay!" Natalie squealed. "Does that mean we get to go to the dance?"

"I think so, as official cupcake bakers," I replied.

"This could get us a lot more customers," Alana said. She straightened her eyeglasses. "We should bring flyers to put out."

"Great idea!" I agreed. "But we have to make sure our cupcakes are amazing. Katie told me that herself."

Ren brushed a strand of blue-streaked hair from her face. "Oh, Emily, you worry too much. When have our cupcakes *not* been amazing?"

Ren had a point. We hadn't been baking cupcakes very long, but they always turned out yummy and looked pretty after our test batch.

Ethan agreed. "Don't forget that your cupcakes won best overall at the Fenton Street baking contest. And you had stiff competition—me!"

We laughed, because we all knew it was true. Ethan and his friends had made pizza cupcakes for the contest.

Our mini cupcakes were chocolate with salted caramel frosting. We thought ours wouldn't win, and we were so nervous! But getting the top prize had been a great feeling.

"We won with a delicious but very safe cupcake," I reminded everyone. "I think we need to be more creative this time."

"Don't worry, Em," Ethan assured me. "We'll come up with something really special for this dance."

I smiled at Ethan. "Can we meet at my mom's house today after school to talk about flavors? And decorating ideas?"

"I have a theater club meeting," Natalie
answered.

Alana frowned. "And I promised Dad
I'd help with Jamie and Kyle while he gets
some work done at home."

"I can come over!" Ren offered.

"Yeah, me too," Ethan said.

I looked at Natalie and Alana. "Is it okay if we meet without you?"

"Sure. Whatever you three come up with will be great," Alana said, and Natalie nodded.

I let out a sigh of happiness. *My friends are the best,* I thought. *With everyone's help, these cupcakes are going to be perfect!*

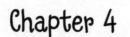

Chapter 4

A Fresh Idea

"Let the brainstorming begin!" Ethan cried. He raised both arms in the air. Ren and I giggled.

"You look like a mad scientist," Ren said.

Ethan sighed. "Sometimes I dream I have a cool science lab with test tubes and bubbling beakers and everything. And I spend all day in there creating new cupcake ideas."

"You sound like my stepsister, Katie," I said. "Cupcakes are all she thinks about most of the time."

"Well, that's a pretty fun thing to think about," Ren said. She took some markers and a notebook out of her backpack. "I have some decorating ideas."

"Let's see!" Ethan said.

Ren opened her notebook. Ethan and I sat up in our chairs to look. The first drawing was a cupcake with yellow frosting and blue jelly beans.

"Blue and yellow, the middle school colors," Ren said.

"Cute," I said. "So, the cupcakes could be lemon and blueberry?"

"Nice," Ethan said. "But not super exciting."

She turned the page. This drawing showed a colorful cupcake with rainbow sprinkles on it.

"That reminds me of an ice-cream cone," I said.

"Could we do an ice cream–flavored cupcake? How would that even work?" Ethan asked. He drummed his hands on the table as he thought. "Freeze-dried ice-cream dots in the batter? But they would melt."

"Okay, what about super-sparkly cupcakes with edible glitter?" Ren offered. She started drawing with metallic markers.

"Cool," Ethan said.

But I shuddered. "Glitter is just so messy! And we need these cupcakes to look really professional."

Then my mom came into the dining room. She carried a tray with three bowls on it. My mom has a job that keeps her really busy. But she started working from home on some of the days that I stay with her. And that's been nice.

"I thought you three might want an after-school snack," Mom said. "I hope nobody has fruit allergies."

She put down a bowl in front of each of us. They were filled with juicy strawberry slices, plump blueberries, tiny orange segments, and chunks of golden pineapple.

"This looks yummy, thank you," Ren bubbled.

"Yeah, thanks, Emily's mom," Ethan said.

Mom laughed. "You can call me Nina," she said.

"I'll let you get back to your meeting," Mom said, and she left us.

We were quiet for a minute as we ate our fruit salad.

"This is so pretty. Like little jewels," Ren remarked.

"And the flavor is really fresh," Ethan said.

An idea popped into my head. "What if we made fresh fruit cupcakes?" I asked. "I know middle schoolers love fruit smoothies. Katie and her friends are always making them."

"That's a great idea!" Ethan said. "I say we do a vanilla cupcake, so the flavor of the fruit can really shine."

"I love this idea," Ren said, sketching.

"We can arrange the fruit on top of the vanilla icing too!"

"I can't wait to hear what Natalie and Alana think," I said.

"They'll love it," Ren promised. "We should make a grocery list, so we can figure out how much they'll cost. Alana is going to want to know that."

EGGS
FLOUR
BLUEBERRIES
STRAWBERRIES
POWDERED SUGAR
SUGAR

"Right," I said, and we worked together to make a list that Ren wrote down in her notebook. Then she tore out the page.

"I'll ask my mom to take me shopping. We'll have to bake the cupcakes on Thursday so they're ready for the dance on Friday," I said.

"I think our brains did a good job storming," Ethan joked.

I smiled. Everything was falling into place. We were going to make Katie and her friends proud!

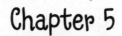

Chapter 5

What's the Big Deal?

Ren's mom came to pick her and Ethan up. Mom agreed to take me shopping for the cupcake ingredients on the way to my dad's house. I was packing my bag when I got a call on my tablet.

"Hey, Natalie," I said. My friend's face appeared on the screen, and I could see she was excited.

"How'd the meeting go?" Natalie asked.

"Great!" I answered. Then I told her our idea. "My mom's taking me ingredient shopping now. Then Thursday we can bake the cupcakes at my dad's house so they'll be ready for the dance on Friday."

"Can I come shopping with you?" Natalie asked.

"Sure," I answered. "We'll pick you up on our way to the store."

When we got to the grocery store, Mom asked, "Okay, what's on your list?"

First, we got some powdered sugar for the frosting. Then we went to the produce section for the fresh fruit.

The stands were filled with plastic cartons of strawberries, blueberries, and raspberries.

"We need two containers of each," I said.

Mom grabbed two cartons of strawberries and put them in our cart. I picked one up and turned it over. I could see one of the berries was a little squished on the bottom. I put the carton back.

"Emily, what are you doing?" Mom asked.

"They need to be perfect, Mom," I said. I picked up another container and examined it. While I did that, Mom put two containers of raspberries in the cart.

"Mom!" I said, putting down one carton and picking up another.

"Look, see how this one is bruised? We need a better box," I said.

But as I went to put it back, Mom took it from my hands.

"Honey, I've been shopping for fruit long before you were born," she said. "These will do just fine."

I felt my cheeks get hot. I stepped behind Mom as she put the rest of the fruit into the cart.

Natalie moved beside me. "Honestly, Em, I don't know why you worry so much."

"These cupcakes have to be perfect," I reminded her. "What if Katie thinks I totally fumbled this order that she trusted me with?"

"Not everything has to be perfect all the time," Natalie said. "It's okay if one strawberry or raspberry is a little funny-looking."

I shrugged. "I can't help it. I like to get things as close to perfect as possible, okay? It's just the way I am."

Mom looked back at us. "What else is on your list?"

We finished shopping and got back in the car.

"Do you want to come to my house for dinner?" Natalie asked.

"No thanks," I said. "I should just go straight to my dad's." I didn't admit it to Natalie, but I was a little hurt by what she'd said. What was the big deal if I liked things to be just right?

We dropped Natalie off. Then Mom brought me to Dad's. They talked while I carefully unpacked the groceries and loaded the fruit into the fridge. I didn't want anything to get squished or tossed around.

Mom came over to kiss me goodbye.
"Love you, sweetie." She looked at Dad.
"Good luck with this one this week."

Dad grinned. "No worries. I'm sure everything will go as perfectly as she wants it to. Right, Em?"

"That's the plan," I said with a sigh.

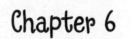

Chapter 6

The Perfect Plan

The next day at school, we discussed our plan for the dance.

"My dad can drive us to the school on Friday with the cupcakes," I told everyone. "And we can do the baking session at Dad's house tomorrow."

Alana showed us a design on her tablet. "What do you think of this flyer? My mom says she can make us fifty copies at work."

We all read the flyer:

DO YOU LIKE MINI CUPCAKES WITH MAXIMUM FLAVOR?

THE MINI CUPCAKE CLUB DELIVERS

The flyer included an email address that Alana's dad had set up for us. And a cute border of tiny cupcakes all around it.

"So adorable!" Ren said.

I honestly thought the border could be a bit bigger. But I remembered what Natalie had said earlier. About me trying too hard to make everything perfect. I didn't want to give her a reason to say that again.

"It's great," I said. *The flyer doesn't have to be perfect,* I thought. *Because the cupcakes will be!*

Do you like mini cupcakes with maximum flavor?

"Oh, and I was thinking," Natalie said, "maybe we could put one of the fruits in the batter."

Ethan jumped in next. "Let's make one batch with strawberries and another with blueberries."

"My stepmom said she'd help me prep the fruit tonight," I said.

"Great! Then we've got a plan," Alana said.

After dinner that night, my stepmom helped me with all the fruit. First, we washed off all the berries and took the tops off the strawberries, then Sharon did the tricky job of carving and coring the pineapple. Next, we pureed some of the strawberries and some of the blueberries, in separate batches, to add to the batter. Sharon also recommended cutting the raspberries and blueberries in small enough pieces to arrange on top of our mini cupcakes. And finally, she sliced up the remaining strawberries and the pineapple rings into little bits for the decorations as well.

When we were finished and everything was stored in the fridge in its own container, I started to wash the cutting board.

"Just leave that, Em," Sharon said with a yawn. "It's getting late."

"Thanks for your help," I said.

She smiled. "No problem. I think your cupcakes are going to be delicious. Everyone's going to love them."

"Really?" I asked.

"Yes, really," she promised.

An hour later, I was in my pajamas, climbing into my comfy bed. I snuggled under my covers and fell asleep. A little while later, I woke to the sound of someone in the kitchen.

My glow-in-the-dark clock showed that it was after midnight. I heard the fridge door open and close.

Must be Dad getting a midnight snack, I thought. *I hope he doesn't bump into the fruit containers!*

Then I fell right back to sleep, totally confident that the cupcakes were going to be amazing.

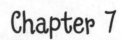

Disaster!

On Thursday afternoon, all the club members assembled at my dad's house. Dad teaches math at Katie's middle school, so we usually get home at the same time and he's able to supervise our baking sessions.

I set up Katie's stand mixer on our big kitchen island. Natalie knew where all the bowls and measuring cups were and got them out of the cabinets.

Alana set up the flour, sugar, salt,

and baking powder. Ren and Ethan got the butter, eggs, and fruit out of the refrigerator.

Outside, rain began to fall.

"There's supposed to be a storm tonight," Alana said with a shiver. "I hate thunder!"

"We should be able to finish all the cupcakes before then," I said.

Ethan started opening up all the containers of fruit in front of him. "Let's start with the blueberry batter," he said, pulling the lid off the blueberries first.

"Oh, I love blueberries!" Ren said. She swiped a piece and popped it in her mouth. She quickly spit it out into a paper towel.

"What's the matter, Ren?" Alana asked.

"I'm not sure," Ren replied. "That blueberry tasted a little . . . off."

I frowned. That wasn't good.

"Maybe it was just a bad berry," Alana said hopefully.

"Impossible," I said. "I picked the very best ones. Try another!"

So Ren tasted another bit. But she made a face and spit that one out too, shaking her head.

"I don't understand," I said. "When we cut up the fruit last night, it was super fresh. Try the other fruit!"

Everyone tried the strawberries, raspberries, and pineapple. It was all sour or mushy!

Then Dad walked in. "What's up, Em? Why all the sad faces?"

"All the fruit seems to have gone bad," I answered. Tears started to well up in my eyes. "I don't understand. It was perfectly fine when Sharon and I put everything in the fridge last night."

"Fruit, in the fridge?" Dad got a cringy look on his face. "Em, I had some fruit last night as a snack. I didn't realize it was for your cupcakes. And when I got up this morning to make breakfast, I noticed I'd left the containers out on the counter."

"All night?" Alana yelped.

"Yes, but I put them back in the fridge this morning," Dad said. "The fruit should be okay, right?"

Ethan was already searching on his tablet. "How long can cut fresh fruit be unrefrigerated?" He groaned as he read the answer. "Once cut or peeled, fresh produce should be refrigerated within two hours. If it is left at room temperature for more than two hours, throw it away."

"Two hours!" I groaned. "This fruit was left out for about seven."

"Oh Em, I'm so sorry," Dad said. He looked like he felt *so* bad. "I had no idea.

It's raining pretty hard now, so let's wait a little bit. Then I'll take you to the store to get more."

I sighed. "I guess we have no choice."

Natalie opened our snack cabinet. "This calls for some microwave popcorn!"

We made the popcorn and ate it cheerlessly, listening to the rain. It got louder and faster. Then we heard the low rumble of thunder.

"Uh-oh," Alana said.

Dad came back into the kitchen. "I looked at the radar. I don't think we should venture out for another two hours," he said. "And by then, you'll all need to get home. We've got frozen pizzas I can make for dinner, but I know that won't help your baking. Can you bake the cupcakes tomorrow after school?"

I started to panic. "No, we can't! The dance starts at five, and there won't be enough time. We have to make them tonight!"

I buried my face in my hands. "The most important cupcake order we've ever had, and we can't fill it!"

Dad sat down next to me and put an arm around my shoulders. "This is all my fault. I am so sorry. Maybe you can make some other kind of cupcakes? Using stuff we already have in the house?"

Ethan stood up, his eyes sparkling. "This is the moment I've been waiting for!" he shouted.

Chapter 8

From Chaos to Calm

"Mr. Green, can we scour the kitchen for ingredients?" Ethan asked.

"Be my guest," my dad answered.

What happened next was chaos! Ethan opened the refrigerator and started shouting out ideas.

"Meat loaf cupcakes?"

"NO!"

"Fried chicken cupcakes?"

"NO!"

"Celery cupcakes?"

"NO!"

Natalie went through all the cabinets. "Soup cans. Pasta sauce. Spaghetti. Maple syrup. Olives . . ."

"Wait!" Ethan said. "What did you say before 'olives'?"

"Um, maple syrup," Natalie repeated.

"We can make French toast cupcakes!" Ethan cried.

Alana searched on her tablet. "I know I've seen a recipe somewhere," she said. "Here it is. Butter, flour, maple syrup, cinnamon, nutmeg. And you can top them with candied bacon."

Dad ran to the fridge. "I know there's turkey bacon in here somewhere!"

"Wait, I hit the jackpot!" Ren cried. She was holding a box of cereal—the kind where each piece looks like a tiny slice of French toast.

"Yessss!" Natalie squealed. "We can put one piece in the center of each cupcake."

Boom! Thunder cracked outside, and we all jumped. Then we laughed.

"I think that's a sign that we're on the right track," I said. "Dad, can you preheat the oven? And we're going to need your help with the bacon."

"On it!" Dad said. He looked so relieved that the problem was solved. As relieved as I felt!

We got to work. Alana and Ren made a vanilla batter spiced with cinnamon and nutmeg. Natalie helped me make the buttercream frosting sweetened with maple syrup. After my dad defrosted the bacon, Ethan showed him how to candy it. They laid the pieces out on a wire rack, then

sprinkled them with brown sugar. The bacon went into the oven at the same time as the cupcakes.

While everything baked, Dad heated up some frozen pizzas in the toaster oven. We munched on it while we waited for everything to cool. Then we worked together to finish the cupcakes. Each one got a swirl of maple frosting, a sprinkle of crispy, crumbled candied bacon, then a topper of French toast cereal.

"Let's leave the bacon off a dozen, for the vegetarians," Ren suggested, and everyone agreed.

When the cupcakes were finished, Natalie cheered. "These are fabulous!"

"They should go in the fridge overnight," Alana said, reading from the recipe.

I looked at Dad. "These are *not* for a midnight snack, understand?"

Dad laughed. "Understood."

Then we all noticed that the rain and thunder had stopped. Dad's phone pinged.

"Looks like your parents are coming to pick you up," he said. "Perfect timing!"

"It ended up being a perfect night after all," I said, smiling at my friends.

All five of us didn't need to deliver the cupcakes on Friday, but we all wanted to. The gymnasium at Park Street School was decorated with blue and yellow lights and balloons when we got there. Music was already thumping.

As we set up our cupcake table, Katie and her Cupcake Club friends—Mia, Alexis, and Emma—gathered around.

"French toast cupcakes!" Emma squealed. "With teeny French toast pieces on top. So cute!"

Alexis picked up one of Alana's flyers. "Great business idea," she said.

Mia picked up a cupcake and sniffed it. "Bacon? Mmm."

Katie put her arm around me. "I knew you'd come up with something amazing, Emily!" I blushed. She sounded really proud.

"Good thing you were staying over at Emma's last night," I told her. "It was chaos!"

"But these look perfect," Katie said.

I looked at Natalie, Alana, Ren, and Ethan. "Yeah, well, that's thanks to my friends."

"Group hug!" Ethan cheered.

And we did. And of course, it was perfect!